The Lucky Star

by Karen Hartman

Based on the life of Joseph A. Hollander and his family

FOR PRODUCTION INQUIRIES

UNITED STATES AND CANADA
info@concordtheatricals.com
1-866-979-0447

UNITED KINGDOM AND EUROPE
licensing@concordtheatricals.co.uk
020-7054-7298

Each title is subject to availability from Concord Theatricals Corp.,
depending upon country of performance. Please be aware that *THE
LUCKY STAR* may not be licensed by Concord Theatricals Corp. in
your territory. Professional and amateur producers should contact the
nearest Concord Theatricals Corp. office or licensing partner to verify
availability.

No one shall make any changes in this title(s) for the purpose of production. No part of this book may be reproduced, stored in a retrieval system, scanned, uploaded, or transmitted in any form, by any means, now known or yet to be invented, including mechanical, electronic, digital, photocopying, recording, videotaping, or otherwise, without the prior written permission of the publisher. No one shall share this title(s), or any part of this title(s), through any social media or file hosting websites.

For all inquiries regarding motion picture, television, online/digital and other media rights, please contact Concord Theatricals Corp.

MUSIC AND THIRD-PARTY MATERIALS USE NOTE

Licensees are solely responsible for obtaining formal written permission from copyright owners to use copyrighted music and/or other copyrighted third-party materials (e.g., artworks, logos) in the performance of this play and are strongly cautioned to do so. If no such permission is obtained by the licensee, then the licensee must use only original music and materials that the licensee owns and controls. Licensees are solely responsible and liable for clearances of all third-party copyrighted materials, including without limitation music, and shall indemnify the copyright owners of the play(s) and their licensing agent, Concord Theatricals Corp., against any costs, expenses, losses and liabilities arising from the use of such copyrighted third-party materials by licensees. For music, please contact the appropriate music licensing authority in your territory for the rights to any incidental music.

IMPORTANT BILLING AND CREDIT REQUIREMENTS

If you have obtained performance rights to this title, please refer to your licensing agreement for important billing and credit requirements.

THE LUCKY STAR (formerly *THE BOOK OF JOSEPH*) was commissioned by Chicago Shakespeare Theater and was developed for Chicago Shakespeare Theater by Rick Boynton, Creative Producer. The world premiere was presented on February 4, 2017 at Chicago Shakespeare Theater in Chicago, Illinois (Barbara Gaines, Artistic Director; Criss Henderson, Executive Director). The production was directed by Barbara Gaines, with scenic design by Scott Davis, costume design by Rachel Healy, lighting design by Philip Rosenberg, and sound design by Miles Polaski and Mikhail Fiksel. The cast was as follows:

RICHARD . . . . Francis Guinan

JOSEPH . . . . Sean Fortunato

MANIA / COURT INTERPRETER / IRIS . . . . Amy J. Carle

KLARA / FELICJA . . . . Gail Shapiro

DOLA / VITA . . . . Patricia Lavery

BERTA / MISS BLAUSTEIN . . . . Glynis Bell

GENKA / YOUNG ARNOLD . . . . Brenann Stacker

LUSIA . . . . Mikey Gray

SALO / COURT OFFICER / STANLEY / ARNOLD . . . . Ron E. Rains

CRAIG . . . . Adam Wesley Brown

The author expresses deep gratitude to the Hollander and Spitzman families.

CHARACTERS

RICHARD – (fifties) A storyteller delivering a book talk about his family. He works the audience, keeping things jovial and sentimental.

Richard doesn't see the other people onstage, primarily his ancestors:

JOSEPH – (35-41) Richard's father and the subject of his story. A leading man. Nickname Joziu [YO zhu].

MANIA – [MAH nia] (late forties) Joseph's eldest sister, has a sardonic side. Also plays **INTERPRETER** and **IRIS** (sixties).

KLARA – [KLAH ra] (early forties) The middle sister, religious. Doubles as **FELICJA** [Fe LEE tzee uh] (late twenties) posh.

DOLA – (39) The youngest of Joseph's older sisters; dramatic, romantic. Doubles as **VITA** [VEE tuh] (29) a warm American in love.

BERTA – [BEAR tuh] (seventies) Family matriarch. Doubles as **MISS BLAUSTEIN** (sixties) a survivor.

GENKA – [GEHN kuh] (17) Klara's eldest daughter, a moody teenager. Doubles as **ARNOLD** (14).

LUSIA – [LOU shuh] (early teens) Genka's cheerful sister.

SALO – [SAH lo] (60) Mania's husband. Also plays **COURT OFFICER, STANLEY DIANA, ELDERLY ARNOLD** (86).

Toward the end of Richard's talk, we meet:

CRAIG – (mid-twenties) Richard's son. A tender smartass.

TIME

Richard's book talk feels like the present, but technically it takes place in more like 2008, shortly after Richard Hollander's book *Every Day Lasts a Year* was published. The technology Richard uses to present the talk shouldn't scream "late aughts!" but should be plausibly backdated for any audience member who gets precise about lining up the dates. Scenes between Joseph and his family take place between 1939-1945.

AUTHOR'S NOTES

Polish-speaking characters use accents only when they are speaking or writing in English. For example, none of the family letters contain accents, nor do Joseph and Felicja's scenes together, but Joseph, Felicja, and Arnold all use accents in the American court.

The Krakow letters, court transcripts, and Elderly Arnold's language are excerpted from documentary material and interviews conducted by the author. Some letters have been reassigned to different family members.

The Krakow letters are published in *Every Day Lasts a Year*, edited by Christopher Browning, Richard Hollander, and Nechama Tec.

Richard and Craig are fictional characters with some basis in biographical facts.

Formatting

A slash (/) indicates overlapping dialogue: the next character starts speaking at the point of the slash.

Thoughts about production

The Lucky Star is a dialogue between past and present, between letters that minimize horrors, and readers and audience members who must burrow between the lines. The letters are vivid and deeply connected to the recipient (usually Joseph) even when the words are spare. A director will find a visual and tonal vocabulary for these letters in which longing and desperation sometimes pop through and sometimes the sentiment is smoothed. Overall, the family in Krakow is more contained at the beginning (1939) and balder at the end (1942).

Richard's area is set up simply, for a book talk. Richard doesn't see the other performers. For example, Richard might show an image of his grandmother Berta before the war, while we see Berta looking more disheveled and upset. Thus the audience sees more that Richard does, at times. In Act Two, Craig and Richard go home suddenly (dare I say magically), and the book talk convention is dropped for the rest of the play. Until then, settings are minimal and fluid.

Don't overplay the drama between Richard and Craig in Act Two, especially Richard's grief. Richard's stakes will never top Joseph's; better to stay grounded and intimate.

Casting thoughts

Depending on the company, Berta may double as Elderly Arnold, and Salo may double as Miss Blaustein, shifting that character to Mr. Blaustein. Additionally, the role of Lusia can be omitted if necessary. Changes available from Samuel French upon request.

ACT ONE

(The audience enters a simple space, arranged for a modest book talk. A video monitor promotes Richard Hollander's book Every Day Lasts a Year: A Jewish Family's Correspondence from Poland.*)*

(With houselights still up, **RICHARD**, *a friendly Jewish American in his fifties, addresses us, the folks who have gathered to hear about this book. A hint of Borscht Belt.)*

RICHARD. Settle in, settle in. I want you to be comfortable. Big things going on tonight.

(A little ad-lib here is okay, "You're gonna want that candy, get it out now," any necessary pre-show information, then:)

A letter is an offering. Time made manifest. A companion. It's not a text, my friends. Not a tweet, nor a snap, nor a swipe. So turn off your phones. Join me back in the twentieth century, when people were here, or there. Not both.

(House lights dim.)

Good evening, *[name of city where we are]*! I'm your humble – you know what, who cares about me? Nothing ever happened to me. Don't even look, okay? I want you to look right through me. I want to be your window. To a past, a time, a tale.

You know I learned something doing research about my father: Everything happens for a reason. Except genocide, amiright?

(He holds up his book.)

7

RICHARD. My book: *Every Day Lasts a Year*! Though tonight's talk will only take a month!

Seriously friends, the moment I found these letters I vowed to shine a light on this family: my aunts, my cousins, my grandmother. Right away I brought them to the Holocaust museum in D.C. and learned that the letters I'm about to share with you are *the most significant correspondence to survive the Krakow Ghetto.*

They are *coherent*: nine members of the Hollander family wrote for two years. They are *robust*: over two hundred letters. And they are nearly *complete*: miraculously my father Joseph Hollander lost almost nothing. I mean he lost…there were losses. But he kept great track of the letters! Numbered them in a little box!

Every Day Lasts a Year: A Jewish Family's Correspondence from Poland was edited by Christopher Browning and Nechama Tec, very big *machers* in the world of Holocaust scholarship. Not that fame matters, my dad used to say, "Be famous among your friends," but it doesn't hurt.

Thanks for coming. I'm amazed anyone showed up at all. Tough sell, the Holocaust. No legs.

    (He looks at his legs.)

There's a joke there but it's beneath me. Badum bum.

You know what has legs? A hero. My father, Joseph Hollander.

For most of history, a letter was how we conjured the missing.

    *(We see **JOSEPH**, late thirties, handsome, iconic, in love. He holds a briefcase. No accent.)*

JOSEPH. Dearest Wife,

I went alone to the nearby forest, lay down on the ground, and read your letters over and over again until it was dark. Letters written by a newlywed girl with love to her husband.

RICHARD. He survives! I don't want you to worry; I want you to enjoy.

JOSEPH. I needed those letters. They warmed up my heart, gave me energy to go through this waiting-period with confidence of our happiness to the end of our days.

If it will happen that I will not have anything to leave to our children, I will give them those first letters.

RICHARD. In memory of my father Joseph Hollander I share with you intimate correspondence, official court transcripts, genuine documented evidence of a hero's quest, on both sides of the Atlantic, to snatch his family from the jaws of annihilation. A universal story of humankind, fleeing persecution for unknown shores.

It's a tale of human triumph! If you stop in the right place.

> *(The Hollander family's elegant apartment in Krakow, Poland, 1939. A joyful night. Joseph's beautifully groomed mother,* **BERTA,** *and sisters,* **MANIA, KLARA,** *and* **DOLA,** *as well as Mania's husband,* **SALO,** *and Klara's daughters,* **GENKA** *and* **LUSIA.** *We see vivid, specific relationships: teasing, dancing, toasting. To a contemporary audience, the scene feels more like "us" than "them.")*

Twenty-eight Gertrudy Street, Krakow. August 1939. The Hollander family home. A large, elegant, urban apartment. Yes, ninety percent of Polish Jews were lower class, religious, shtetl people, but the Hollanders were the ten percent.

We have the matriarch Berta Hollander, the eldest sister Mania and her husband Salo. The middle sister Klara married a man called Dawid *[DUH vid]* – he didn't write much – they have two teenagers Genka and Lusia. And the youngest of the sisters is Dola. Classy people. Not Anatevka, think Central Park West.

I imagine them late summer 1939, celebrating. Who knows what they're celebrating? It is Before.

(Inside the house, perhaps someone plays an instrument while others sing a Polish tune of the day [crooner, not Klezmer].*)

RICHARD. Joseph was a successful lawyer and a pioneer in the travel business. He had an apartment with a marble lobby. A socialite for a wife. And because he traveled, he saw.

In March of 1939 Hitler's army entered Czechoslovakia, occupied Austria, and the Western powers *did not react*.

Now Joseph confronts his family. Eight miles east of Hitler and his army. So obvious. To us.

(JOSEPH enters the party in hero mode.)

BERTA. Join in dear Joziu, we miss your baritone!

JOSEPH. Wonderful news! I chartered a train for a wealthy man named Spitzman and his family. In the bargain, he agreed to hold seats for all of you. I secured visas to Portugal. We are saved! We leave tonight!

(Beat. The FAMILY finds JOSEPH a little much.)

BERTA. What an extraordinary effort, my darling boy.

JOSEPH. Yes it was.

BERTA. But you must admit it's quite sudden.

JOSEPH. The invasion is sudden. Occupation will be sudden. Since last fall, I have sought homes all over the world for the Jews marched out of Germany with bayonets at their backs. Arranged papers for Panama, Cuba, Nicaragua, the corners of the globe. For us, I have visas *in Europe*.

BERTA. My son is a marvel. Helping others, helping his family...

---

*A license to produce *The Book of Joseph* does not include a performance license for any third-party or copyrighted music. Licensees should create an original composition or use music in the public domain. If licensees are not able to do this, the playing and/or singing is optional. For further information, please see Music Use Note on page 3.

JOSEPH. The subject is not your son the marvel; the subject is *we must leave*. Mania. Salo. Set an example. Off we go.

MANIA. I'm an old lady, almost fifty. Salo is sixty.

SALO. Let's wait and see.

JOSEPH. The Nazis want all Jews out of the Reich, and now the Reich expands into Poland. What chaos and violence are you waiting to see?

KLARA. You'll scare the girls.

JOSEPH. Consider your girls!

KLARA. School starts this week. Lusia finally has the photography course she's been begging for.

LUSIA. And my own camera!

GENKA. Mama can I go? I don't have a stupid camera.

KLARA. Genka, shh. God has been so good to us.

JOSEPH. So far, but let's not test Him.

KLARA. I have faith we'll find a way; why turn our good life upside down?

> (**JOSEPH** *turns a wineglass upside down. It spills.* **GENKA** *is thrilled. No one shares Joseph's fear.*)

GENKA. Uncle Joziu!

JOSEPH. Life is upside down! German troops mass ON OUR BORDER a day's march away! All they need to do is step!

BERTA. Joziu, it was never easy to be a Jew. You had to stand in the back all through university. Your father bless his memory stayed strong when hoodlums yanked his beard.

JOSEPH. The hoodlums are now the government.

MANIA. We don't know anything for sure.

JOSEPH. Last November, all over Germany "hoodlums" smashed, looted, and burned every Jewish business. Torched old-age homes with the people locked inside. Shut men in synagogues overnight, forced them to piss the walls.

KLARA. Language.

JOSEPH. Citizens and paramilitary did most of the work, Nazis whispered support. Now they are here.

DOLA. I'll go.

JOSEPH. Yes! Dola! I booked us all into a spa in Romania. From there to Rome, and eleven visas to Lisbon.

DOLA. I could use a spa.

JOSEPH. Right, we're not really going to the spa...

DOLA. I know. I have a sense of humor.

KLARA. I'll get your suitcase.

> *(She exits.)*

BERTA. *(To* **DOLA.***)* What about your husband?

DOLA. Henek went to his mother in Russia.

BERTA. He is seeking opportunities for you both.

DOLA. Is he? Mother why don't we go with Joziu?

JOSEPH. That's right! That's right! And Mania, say yes. You and Salo have time. Let your grief go, start new in Portugal.

MANIA. How does Felicja feel about your entire family piling along?

BERTA. Oh, I don't wish to burden your lovely wife.

JOSEPH. She wants you with us, naturally.

MANIA. You were a terrible liar even as a boy. Your cheek twitches.

JOSEPH. Felicja understands the situation. It's not a dinner party. Of course we would invite you to a dinner party...

DOLA. *(To* **JOSEPH.***)* She looks at me judge-y.

MANIA. She's going to look at you judge-y the whole way to Lisbon. She doesn't even trust us with her dining table. Wrote a *megillah* about how to polish. She thinks we never owned furniture?

JOSEPH. None of this matters!

> *(***DOLA*** feels caught, but not tragically so. This trip sounds exciting. On the other hand, the sister-in-law.)*

DOLA. I don't want to be a burden.

MANIA. Dola, you have to learn when you're not wanted. That's your trouble with men.

DOLA. Mother and Mania are right. I'm a married woman. I'm not free.

JOSEPH. But you said you would come!

DOLA. Goodbye Joziu.

JOSEPH. I got you all tickets and papers. No one has tickets and papers. It was impossible and I did it!

BERTA. You'll help us another time. You always find a way my precious boy, my treasure.

SALO. We need time to plan.

BERTA. You be safe, my dear child. May the lucky star never leave you.

> *(She kisses* **JOSEPH.** *He holds the kissed spot, his lucky star.)*

JOSEPH. Come with me. Come with me. COME WITH ME!

> *(The* **FAMILY** *recedes. The Krakow apartment goes dark.)*

RICHARD. The Nazis invade Poland a couple days later, just as Joseph predicted. German fliers circle, gunning down refugees for sport. The Hollanders, without papers or tickets, join the hordes of Polish Jews trying to walk east, to Russia.

> *(***JOSEPH** *and the elegantly dressed* **FELICJA** *ride a train. An oasis, especially to her.)*

FELICJA. Is there meal service?

JOSEPH. We are fleeing.

FELICJA. But surely there will be staff?

RICHARD. Joseph and Felicja approach Rome.

> *(***FELICJA** *applies lipstick.)*

FELICJA. How will I replace this shade?

JOSEPH. There will be lipstick in Portugal.

FELICJA. But I am a blonde.

JOSEPH. Hand me your earrings.

FELICJA. My diamonds?

JOSEPH. They might help us cross the Italian border.

FELICJA. These were my *birthday present.*

JOSEPH. *(Dry.)* It is a time of untold sacrifice.

RICHARD. Joseph's family is trying to escape through Russia, but before they make it to the border, the Soviet Union invades from the East. Stalin's secret pact with Hitler, 1939? Did anyone study this? Only *two weeks* after they missed their chance with Joseph, my family was sealed in Poland, caught from both sides.

> *(Perhaps we see the* **FAMILY** *straggling with their belongings.* **RICHARD** *might pull us away from this image.)*

They tried to go home. They were robbed on the way back, and of course that elegant apartment was stripped.

But I promised you letters! That's what you're here for! Letters, letters, letters!

First one is a good one! My grandmother, Berta Hollander, November 1939.

> *(The first letter.* **BERTA** *is warm, yearning for her son.)*

BERTA. My dear and beloved Joziu and Felicja!

I wish you much good fortune wherever you turn. I can't express myself with words. I am content with everything; I only ask God to give me life to see you again.

(Merciless.) When one suffers, I say *at least it is not my son.*

RICHARD. Sweet lady, my grandmother. Now Dola, the youngest of Joseph's elder sisters:

> *(The* **FAMILY**'s *clothes look worse, hair hasn't been styled, but they are okay.)*

DOLA. Thank God we are all healthy and we work. Henek remains in Russia with his family. I too intend to go to Uncle Tolstoy.

RICHARD. Klara, the middle sister:

KLARA. My dear, I just want this winter to pass so the sun can warm us up again. Lusia takes private sewing lessons and Genka got a job where she gets a salary and is very proud of that.

> (*A glimpse of the girls together,* **GENKA** *boastful.*)

They come home together. Our biggest pleasure now is to sit at home.

RICHARD. Now – here it's neat, with the help of my scholarly team I've begun to reconcile what's *in* the letters with what's *not* in the letters. Remember they had to pass through censors.

DOLA. (*A fake letter, super bright tone.*) Dear Joziu,
On the way back to Krakow, German soldiers beat us, made Salo clean shit with his bare hands, and probed Mother's vagina for money.
Kisses, Dola.

RICHARD. I'm not saying that happened, but if it *had* happened, you wouldn't know from the letters. Remember how this collection is nearly complete, despite the fact that the Nazis read every word and *decided* whether to deliver each letter? The Hollanders were masters of omission and understatement. When Dola writes:

DOLA. I went through lots of changes.

RICHARD. She means the Nazi flag raised over the city, the seizure of Jewish-owned vehicles, Jews forced into slave labor, the creation of a Jewish police squad to impose the new laws, et cetera. All within two months of the invasion. Mania, the eldest sister, explains:

MANIA. From tomorrow we will wear uniforms. I suspect we will look quite fine in them.

RICHARD. Which means –

> *(The* **FAMILY,** *in unison, puts on yellow stars.)*

You probably figured that out. You look like a bright group. Not informed necessarily, but bright.

MANIA. We have become like a herd of chickens now; we sit and warm our butts at the stove.

RICHARD. Her husband Salo:

SALO. There is not much to relate about the business; it goes slowly and in small steps.

BERTA. My much-loved children,

Today I received your letter and card, and I am in a hurry to give you news.

> *(The silence of not giving news.)*

KRAKOW FAMILY. We are all comfortable.

RICHARD. When I found the letters they were stamped with swastikas. That's a bit chilling. What was he doing with swastikas, my Jewish father who survived the war? But of course Poland was suddenly under the Third Reich, so letters got stamped with swastikas like our letters are stamped with little flags. The regime change didn't mean anything. Except loss of freedom, stability, basic personal rights. We'll call it Phase One.

> *(The* **FAMILY** *is experiencing discomfort but not dread. And it brings them joy to communicate to Joseph, so the tone stays bright.)*

DOLA. I live already in the third apartment, and soon I have to move to a fourth one. But do not worry about us! We are healthy and this is the most important thing.

BERTA. If only winter were over. The main thing for me is to get a letter from you. I read your letters several times so that I remember them. I think about you day and night, my dear ones.

KLARA. *(Whisper – a rare instance where tone communicates urgency.)* Our *neighbors* are horrible people; they make lots of noise not only during the day but they also don't let us sleep at night. My husband has announced he is moving us to Uncle Tolstoy!

RICHARD. Okay this is neat – my middle son Craig figured it out when he was just an undergraduate – Uncle Tolstoy means Russia! Craig got very into this. Obsessed.

KLARA. But there are certain difficulties connected with that.

RICHARD. "Difficulties." It's the Hollander denial that got these letters through.

KLARA. *(Normal voice.)* Lusia sews really nicely now. We need it badly because during our trip we lost two suitcases with dresses.

RICHARD. "Trip," the futile attempt to flee. "Lost."

KLARA. We greet you warmly. Stay well and happy.

MANIA. I would give my life away to know if you are doing well.

DOLA. I am breathing but I am not alive.

RICHARD. I guess they let that one go.

DOLA. Felicja's bedroom and dining room sets are being kept in good condition. A hundred times a day I thank God that you are where you are.

GENKA. *(Still a whiny middle-class kid.)* Dear Uncle,
You won't imagine how much I would like to be with you. This climate makes me feel very bad.

RICHARD. Teenagers.

GENKA. I am sitting all day long in the store, and I really want to learn some profession. I think about photography or retouching. How do you like this idea? I would so much like to meet with you and talk. Write back to us a long letter since we are so curious how you are doing. Kisses, Genka.

RICHARD. This was supposed to be the Wait and See phase, but they didn't have to wait long. Reality doesn't melt, it collapses in chunks. The Hollanders seem to be living together now, except Dola who keeps renting rooms. And where is Joseph by the end of 1939?

(**JOSEPH**, *his nice coat much worse for the journey, pleads for his life. Thick Polish accent. We suddenly see our hero as a refugee. Errors sic.*)

JOSEPH. Ellis Island, December 22, 1939.

RICHARD. Now here is a *document*!

JOSEPH. To Mrs. Franklin D. Roosevelt, the White House, Washington D.C.

RICHARD. Eleanor Roosevelt! He doesn't even speak *English* so who knows how he did this!

JOSEPH. My Dear Madam –

Please pardon my troubling you, by asking you for help, but your well-known noble-mindedness and our tragic situation will excuse us.

RICHARD. Brains and balls! That was my dad! Listen close, I couldn't make this stuff up. I didn't make this stuff up. Not. One. Word.

JOSEPH. We are Jews, Polish subjects, who were obliged to leave Poland on account of the last accidents.

After three long months wandering through Rumania, Yugoslavia, and Italy, we got Portuguese visas in Rome and left for Lisboa with the ship *Vulcania*.

Unfortunately, Portuguese authorities did not let us land, without explaining the reason, and we were compelled to come with the same ship to New York.

It threatened us the deportation to Germany, because in Italy we signed that we won't come back anymore, under the menace of deportation to Polish frontier.

We should have been lost, if American authorities would not allow for us staying on Ellis Island till our trial, which will take place on the twenty-sixth instant in the court in New York.

We don't know how will be the verdict of the court, because we have nor American, neither any other visas. And that is why we are begging you – Dear Madam – for help.

We beg don't send us back to Germany, because that means death for us. Let us stay through a shortest time in America, just to equipoise our teared-to-pieces nerves.

We won't be public charge because we have money to support us.

The undersigned thirty-five-year-old, director of one of the biggest travel-offices in Poland

> (**FELICJA** *and* **ARNOLD** *appear with him.*)

with his twenty-eight years old wife Felicja and fourteen years old boy Arnold Spitzman whom we are protecting, the son of a Polish aviator

> (*Secret from* **ARNOLD.**)

who was killed in the first days of the war.

> (*End secret.*)

Three creatures beg you:

FELICJA, ARNOLD & JOSEPH. *(Polish accents.)* Dear Madam – save us!

JOSEPH. And don't let send us back from this free American country to Germany. We believe in your nobility and are now living with the hope that our appell will be granted.

We remain. Yours very truly. Joseph Hollander.

FELICJA. With wife.

RICHARD. *(Delighted, almost manic.)* I found all this in my dad's file at the National Archives. Oh yeah, my dad has a *file*. A box. About four hundred pages. Joseph Hollander became a test case – would the U.S. admit European Jewish refugees, or not? It's only 1939, so "wait and see" is happening all over. But the problem with waiting...

Anyhow! I found this note from Eleanor Roosevelt's office that arrived to the Immigration and Naturalization Service just five days later – December 27, with Christmas in between. The postal service was crackerjack back then!

The note says, "In answering, please say you are doing so at Mrs. Roosevelt's request." Eleanor Roosevelt read Dad's letter!

Meanwhile, the Krakow family thinks Joseph is all set.

SALO. January 1, 1940.

Dear Joziu, I am very happy because of what you write. It's great that you got a permanent stay permit and a work permit.

RICHARD. He had neither.

DOLA. Thank God you don't have to wander anymore!

RICHARD. He was stateless, homeless, jobless, a prisoner on Ellis Island waiting to be sent wherever the U.S. could fling him.

LUSIA. Don't worry. God is with us.

DOLA. Maybe in a few years you will become an American millionaire.

RICHARD. Did the family think he was Superman? The *pressure*, to save his family in Europe, his wife, his ward. Joseph doesn't even speak the language. Yet he wrangles a day in court. I got the transcript!

> (*Courtroom. A* **COURT OFFICER** *and an aggressive* **INTERPRETER**. *This hearing is not pro forma, but a vicious attempt to smear the defendants.*)

OFFICER. Hearing before a Board of Special Inquiry held at Ellis Island, New York Harbor, New York, January 26, 1940.

To the elder male alien: What is your full and correct name?

INTERPRETER. (*Direct Polish translation of the* **OFFICER**'s *questions.*) *Jakie jest pana pełne i poprawne imię i nazwisko?*

JOSEPH. Jozef Artur Hollander.

OFFICER. How old are you?

INTERPRETER. *Ile ma pan lat?*

JOSEPH. *Trzydzieści pięc.*

INTERPRETER. Thirty-five.

OFFICER. Of what country are you a citizen?

INTERPRETER. *Jakiego kraju jest pan obywatelem?*

JOSEPH. *Polski.*

INTERPRETER. Poland.

OFFICER. What is your race?

INTERPRETER. *Jaka jest pana rasa?*

JOSEPH. *Hebrajczyk.*

INTERPRETER. Hebrew.

RICHARD. Shocking that the United States would ask about race or religion in an immigration hearing! But it's here. Picture the court officer and the interpreter, two against one.

> (*A visual alignment of the* **COURT OFFICER** *with the* **INTERPRETER** *suggests they are both cross-examining* **JOSEPH**, *though we only hear the questions in English.*)

INTERPRETER & OFFICER. You have the right to have a relative or friend present at this hearing.

INTERPRETER. Do you wish to avail yourself of this right?

JOSEPH. No.

INTERPRETER. When were you last in Poland?

JOSEPH. We all left Poland together, September 15, 1939.

INTERPRETER. You mean yourself, wife, and the person you claim as a ward, Arnold Spitzman?

JOSEPH. I left with my wife, and my ward left with his relatives, but we all left the same time.

INTERPRETER. Was it approximately fifteen days after Germany entered Poland that you left?

JOSEPH. Yes.

OFFICER. (*Aggressive.*) Why did you leave?

JOSEPH. To save our lives.

INTERPRETER. To what country did you go?

JOSEPH. Rumania.

OFFICER. How long did you stay in Rumania?

JOSEPH. About eight days.

INTERPRETER. To what country did you go next?

JOSEPH. Via Yugoslavia to Italy.

OFFICER. Why did you go to Italy?

JOSEPH. It was the only place where a citizen of Poland could enter without being in possession of any visas.

INTERPRETER. How long has this boy been in your care?

JOSEPH. Since November 24, 1939.

INTERPRETER. Do you know his parents?

JOSEPH. I only saw his parents once in Krakow.

RICHARD. And yet he takes responsibility for the child! We don't know what happened to Arnold Spitzman but we know what *would* have happened, in Poland.

OFFICER. On what date did you board the SS Vulcania?

JOSEPH. The twenty-sixth of November, 1939.

OFFICER. What was your destination?

JOSEPH. To Lisbon, Portugal.

INTERPRETER. On what country's passports did you travel?

JOSEPH. On Polish passports.

INTERPRETER. Were the passports visaed for travel to Portugal?

JOSEPH. Yes.

INTERPRETER. Were they visaed for travel to any other country?

JOSEPH. No.

INTERPRETER & OFFICER. Were they visaed for travel to the United States?

JOSEPH. No.

OFFICER. Were you permitted to land in Lisbon?

JOSEPH. No, I was rejected.

INTERPRETER & OFFICER. Why were you rejected?

JOSEPH. As much as I could understand, that they didn't honor my Polish passport and my visa to Portugal.

OFFICER. What was your purpose in going to Portugal?

JOSEPH. Just seeking refuge until we will be able to return to our own country.

INTERPRETER. When you were refused admission at Lisbon, Portugal, why didn't you return to Naples, Italy?

JOSEPH. I could not because I left Italy, signing a document that I will not return there.

INTERPRETER. Why didn't you go to some other European country?

JOSEPH. I tried and I could not obtain a visa!

INTERPRETER & OFFICER. *(The big question – they suspect he was trying to come to the U.S. all along.)* When you left Naples, Italy, was it your intention to come to the United States?

JOSEPH. Not at that time.

OFFICER. Is the part of Poland where you last resided now occupied by Germany?

JOSEPH. Yes.

INTERPRETER. Will you return to Poland if Germany continues that occupation?

JOSEPH. No.

OFFICER. Have you a fixed, permanent domicile anywhere at the present time?

JOSEPH. No.

OFFICER. Has your wife?

JOSEPH. No.

OFFICER. Has your ward?

JOSEPH. No.

INTERPRETER & OFFICER. Where do you hope to make your future home?

JOSEPH. The only hope I have is that the war will end and that I will be able to return to my home.

OFFICER. Do you mean Poland?

JOSEPH. Yes.

INTERPRETER. Have you relatives in the U.S.?

JOSEPH. I have none; my wife has.

INTERPRETER. Have you finances in the U.S. apart from the twenty-eight dollars you have with you?

JOSEPH. Yes! With my wife's cousin in Brooklyn, New York. I have over $4,000.

>   *(That's a suspicious amount of money.)*

INTERPRETER. Is it your money?

JOSEPH. Yes.

INTERPRETER. What is the source of this money?

JOSEPH. I transferred the money to him through London, England, where I had the money before.
(A little proud.) I kept my money in London.

INTERPRETER. Have you evidence that your "wife's cousin" has over $4,000, belonging to you?

JOSEPH. No.

OFFICER. To the minor Alien Boy!

>   (**ARNOLD SPITZMAN**, *a terrified fourteen-year-old boy. Polish accent.*)

INTERPRETER & OFFICER. What is your name?

ARNOLD. Arnold Spitzman?

INTERPRETER. *(Cruel, she knows his father is dead.)* Is your father living?

>   (**ARNOLD** *asks himself that question night and day.*)

ARNOLD. I don't know.

INTERPRETER. When did you last see your father?

ARNOLD. About ten days before the war broke out. He was in the army and he came home to visit the family.

INTERPRETER. With what troops was your father?

ARNOLD. *(Obviously.)* Polish troops.

INTERPRETER. What is your father's name?

ARNOLD. Maximilian Spitzman.

INTERPRETER. Of what country is your father a citizen?

ARNOLD. *(Obviously.)* Poland.

INTERPRETER. Why did you leave your mother in Poland?

ARNOLD. My father was in the Polish army, and my mother had a store which she attempted to liquidate, and in the meantime she sent me and my younger sister, age seven, to my aunt and uncle Spitzman who resided at Lvov, Poland, and I was on my way with them to Portugal.

OFFICER. Were you acquainted with Mr. and Mrs. Hollander before you left Poland?

ARNOLD. Yes.

(A decent lie.) They came frequently to our home in Krakow, Poland.

(The **COURT OFFICER** *notes the discrepancy with Joseph's statement.* **JOSEPH** *cringes.)*

INTERPRETER. How did you become attached to them?

ARNOLD. I left Poland with my uncle and aunt about ten days after the outbreak of the war in Poland. I went with them to Bologna, Italy, where I was taken ill with typhus and was in a hospital for about four weeks. When I recovered, my uncle and aunt were either in Paris or on the way to Paris, and I returned to Rome and joined the Hollanders, who knew me.

INTERPRETER. Why didn't you go to Paris to join your uncle and aunt?

ARNOLD. My uncle and aunt went to Paris in order to go to Lisbon, Portugal and I was supposed to meet them there. But I was not permitted to land in Lisbon, Portugal, where my family was waiting.

INTERPRETER & OFFICER. What are your plans for your future residence?

ARNOLD. I don't know.

OFFICER. To the elder male alien:

If the boy is admitted to the U.S., do you guarantee to support him, take care of him, shelter him, and see that he doesn't become a public charge to the government or any division thereof?

JOSEPH. Yes.

OFFICER. Did you accept this obligation to him at the time he started to travel in your company?

JOSEPH. Yes.

INTERPRETER. What obligation have you to support or take care of this boy?

JOSEPH. Just human interest.

RICHARD. Human. Interest. Wouldn't you be fighting to save your own skin?

FELICJA. *(To* **JOSEPH,** *cautioning about Arnold.)* Joziu...

OFFICER. Testimony from the female alien has not been summoned.

FELICJA. *(Thick, broken English.)* Yes, please.

INTERPRETER. *(To* **JOSEPH.***)* If admitted, could you, or anyone interested in your behalf, deposit bonds in the sum of $500 for each of you, to guarantee to the government that you would leave the U.S. within a stated, definite time?

JOSEPH. Yes!

INTERPRETER. In the case of the minor applicant, if it were required, could you deposit a further bond to guarantee he would not become a public charge in the U.S.?

JOSEPH. Yes!

INTERPRETER. Is there any further evidence you wish to present with regard to your application for admission to the U.S.?

JOSEPH. I beg for the sake of humanity to grant us a refuge here as we have no other place to go at this time.

RICHARD. *(As if a prayer.)* I beg for the sake of humanity.

To grant us a refuge here.

As we have no other place to go at this time.

Who among us might need to respond to those words one day?

Or say those words?

OFFICER. Because you are aliens not in possession of appropriate, unexpired, consular immigration visas:

OFFICER & INTERPRETER. The board has voted to deny you admission into the United States under Section 13 of the Immigration Act of 1924.

INTERPRETER. You have the right of appeal. Do you wish to appeal?

JOSEPH. I wish to appeal.

RICHARD. Berta writes to Felicja's brother:

> (**BERTA** *is trying to cover, but begging. We begin to see her desperation.*)

BERTA. Dear Mr. Schreiber:

Please excuse me for turning to you, but I do not know my son's address, as he has not yet written to me.

RICHARD. Of course he was writing. But for months nothing got through.

BERTA. I am very concerned about him. And so I am enlisting your kindness and hoping that you will answer my letter right away. Thank you in advance. Yours truly, B. Hollander.

And Mr. Schreiber, should Joziu read the letter, I ask him to write to me himself and give me his exact address, and I will write him a long letter. I send kisses to both. Felicja can also write me a few lines. I will be very happy if she is content.

Your mother.

RICHARD. Oh right, Felicja had a brother Jan Schreiber who was a lawyer in New York. He housed them temporarily and argued their case. Minor support.

This is a story about one man making a difference and that man is Joseph Hollander!

> (**FELICJA** *and* **ARNOLD** *enter Felicja's brother's magnificent apartment.*)

ARNOLD. Your brother lives here? Wowie.

FELICJA. Don't touch anything and don't ask what anything costs.

ARNOLD. No, ma'am.

FELICJA. Are you hungry?

ARNOLD. Yes, ma'am!

FELICJA. Go to the park and buy a hot dog.

>   (**ARNOLD** *looks blank.*)

My brother is returning soon. Joseph is at the court and the post office. It would be a good time for you to be elsewhere.

ARNOLD. I have no money.

>   (**FELICJA** *gives him a coin.*)

Thank you.

>   (*He looks longingly around the living room and goes.*)

FELICJA. This is not going to work, Joziu.

RICHARD. February 1940. The same month as admission was denied:

>   (**SALO** *is flooded with feelings that he holds back under normal circumstances.*)

SALO. I want to hope we will see each other again. I would really like that very much. We did not say a proper goodbye. Here huge –

RICHARD. Illegible –

SALO. – Held sway that was –

RICHARD. Illegible –

SALO. – Necessary. We send warm regards. Write us the most detailed letter you can. Business still exists under an Aryan leadership.

MANIA. (*Comforting* **SALO** *while communicating to* **JOSEPH.**) We are not better or worse off than thousands of others in similar situations and relationships. We can come to work, while many other business owners lost everything and cannot even enter their old locales.

SALO. That's so to say a plus for us. With an affectionate hug and many kisses. Your Salo.

MANIA. I would like to ask you countless questions, but not this time. I am just asking you to write often, it's going to be the only pleasure for us in these difficult days. Dear Mother is well. Even if we try hard we cannot replace you for her.

BERTA. My dear and beloved children!

(Terrified.) I really do not know what I should write you...in the next letter I will have my wits more about me and will write more.

JOSEPH. *(Frantically to the group.)* Jewish agencies who help my case tell me that the American government is just waking up to the situation of masses of Jews in Europe who need to immigrate. The noose will tighten. Quotas are decreasing not increasing in response to the plight of European Jews, precisely because there are millions of you. Us. America fears an invasion. Move now. Do *not* seek permission to stay in Krakow. Do *not* weigh the cost.

(Whispers.) Forget Felicja's dining set.

(The **FAMILY** *listens.)*

Mother, Dola, Klara, Genka, Lusia, Dawid, Mania, Salo. Move! I stand ready to help you in every way available to me and some that are not. I will cross the ocean. I will crush mountains. Move!

RICHARD. Early 1940, Dad scrambles to buy more time by getting his appeal, month after month. Felicja's lawyer brother helped a bit there. Through it all, Dad never forgets the ones at home! Call this Phase Two: Joseph tries to get the family out, while the family hunkers down.

JOSEPH. March 16, 1940.

Dear Dr. Samuel Spann,

I am a brother-in-law of Dawid Wimisner *[VIH-mihz-ner]* from Krakow, and I am writing on his and my sister Klara's behalf.

RICHARD. Dad was ordered deported a month before this letter! Yet he writes on Dawid and Klara's behalf! What a mensch! Did I mention how many people he helped escape in the 1930s before he had to flee? Dad was a travel agent and undaunted by red tape.

JOSEPH. I keep receiving letters from my sister and my brother-in-law from Krakow, and from the content, I can easily guess that the situation over there is terrible.

> (*The* **FAMILY** *looks worse. Literally and figuratively threadbare. The tone of these letters is blunt.*)

MANIA. We have very warm days but we sit at home, since no one likes to walk in Krakow anymore.

JOSEPH. I have to do absolutely everything in order to help them to leave.

SALO. I ask you in my own and Mania's name not to send packages anymore. They are not reaching us. Also for other reasons I don't think it's a good idea.

JOSEPH. I have an opportunity to arrange their emigration to Cuba or Mexico. It will require a very significant amount of money.

KLARA. The more I get to know people, the more I treasure dogs.

JOSEPH. I also have to purchase four ship's tickets.

DOLA. I rent a small room where I live now. I learn English; I signed up for lessons. I cut fabric if there is anything to cut. And I wait.

JOSEPH. I know from my brother-in-law that he gave you power of attorney to collect the money he had in the Chankin Society.

MANIA. We all sit like on a volcano. Our nerves are almost used up.

JOSEPH. Please send me as soon as possible all the necessary information about the amount of money my sister Klara and her husband can dispose of.

BERTA. May God help at least you be the lucky one.

JOSEPH. Knowing you from Poland I have no doubts that you will do everything in order to help me to save my sister and her family. I am awaiting your response with

impatience since the situation is burning and any delay
may be catastrophic.

RICHARD. I sometimes ask myself, WWJD? What Would
Joseph Do?

> (*He shows his hand, where it's written in
> ink.*)

It's just pen. I want a tattoo, but Craig says I might
regret it when I'm an adult.

KLARA. Dear Mother was sick but you don't need to be
surprised by this. *Now* we can write that we were very
worried.

RICHARD. Everyone protects everyone else from information.
It's the Hollander way.

BERTA. Dear child, you do not need to be concerned about
my illness, since I have been very well for a long time
now, and as the saying goes, better to have been sick
than to have been rich.

I would like to write you all day long, I believe I am
talking with you. I cannot write much about myself,
I would not have enough paper to write everything
down. Thank God for everything, that we can walk
about. The winter was very hard. We lived in the hope
that the sun would shine again, and we could breathe
a sigh of relief.

DOLA. Henek is still at his mother's. I live in a rented room
and wait for the end of this war. I eat dinners at Klara's.
She also took two children of refugees who come for
dinners. If I knew that I could be back with my family
whenever I wanted to I would have gone to Uncle
Tolstoy. I am sure I would find work over there.

MANIA. Dola fools herself that over there she would find
a job. That's wrong. She is not made for working. She
doesn't have a profession or qualifications and it's
difficult to start something new when you are forty
years old.

I do not blame her, she has honest enthusiasm but there
is nothing to do at this time. There is simply no work.

The worst is that Dear Mother worries about her so
much. She has little news from Henek, he writes only
about himself. He doesn't even ask how Dola supports
herself. She learned from somebody that he is doing
very well over there.

KLARA. This old aunt of ours is horrible, thank God you
don't know her personally. She was always impossible,
but now one has to be very strong-minded around her,
in order to tolerate her demands. I feel sorry for the
people she lives with.

(**RICHARD** *stays upbeat, the host.*)

RICHARD. The "old aunt" is Germany! Craig again! Sharp
kid!

MANIA. We write in German because of the censors.

(*To herself.*) *Heil* censors!

KLARA. Your letters are like a nectar for us. We get drunk
on them. You write that you feel bad you cannot help
us. I assure you we're lacking nothing and may God
allow that it will stay like this till the end of the war.

I had a dream that you came and tears of joy were
floating down my cheeks.

LUSIA. God allow that we will see each other in happiness.

GENKA. You asked how I am doing after the surgery for my
appendicitis.

RICHARD. He kept track of his niece's appendix! I don't
know which of my own kids has their tonsils.

GENKA. After two weeks I could already play football. I
have an ugly scar but it doesn't matter. I usually don't
walk around with this part of the body exposed.

We have a beautiful summer but I don't go to the
swimming pool for obvious reasons.

RICHARD. Jews were already forbidden from swimming in
public pools. And yet FDR and the U.S. Immigration
Department wanted to send Joseph and his family, and
countless others, *back to Poland*. Nothing to fear but
fear itself. And Jews. And Japanese Americans. And...
you fill in the blank.

DOLA. Please write me honestly how you feel. If you want to whisper something into my ear, please do.

JOSEPH. *(Whispers.)* I'm frightened. Dola, I'm so frightened!

KLARA. I have only one prayer now: wherever you go, whatever you do, may the lucky star always be above your head.

KRAKOW FAMILY. I have only one prayer now: wherever you go, whatever you do, may the lucky star always be above your head.

MANIA. For my fiftieth birthday I received an original gift: five people from Poznan came to share my apartment, including the use of the kitchen.

GENKA. Thanks for remembering my birthday; it's really nice of you!! I am so proud of you! Everybody envies me that I have relatives in America. And what relatives they are! Kisses!

> *(She makes kisses.* **MANIA** *locks eyes with* **JOSEPH**. *It's raw.)*

MANIA. My dearest brother –

Should I thank you for a long beautiful letter or for the birthday wishes or for the package you sent?

I thank you for all of that.

As you remember, I turned half a century on July 19. What did I experience? Nothing and a lot.

I married being twenty, didn't know anything about life and people, and a year after I already had a child. A child had a child. My parenting responsibilities took over, maybe it was better this way, I didn't have much time to think.

But he, too, disappeared forever. Only everlasting emptiness stayed.

I know my dear brother that you, despite your young age, went through a lot.

Many times it hurt me really much that you didn't find a way to me. You thought I am stupid, or you preferred to deal with all the difficulties by yourself. But I had for you, my dear boy, not only sisterly feelings, but my eyes can look deeply into your soul. I knew that the office job was not the only and entire reason for your nervous breakdown.

RICHARD. Nervous breakdown?

MANIA. Sometimes I feel like somebody asked me to sing after my tongue was removed.

> *(The intimacy is too much. She breaks* **JOSEPH**'s *gaze.)*

Thank you for the package; it contained coffee, tea, oil which made me very happy but we can get everything here. Milk wasn't there but we can get fresh milk every day. The women bring it like they used to before the war.

> *(***JOSEPH***,* **FELICJA,** *and* **ARNOLD** *stand before* **STANLEY DIANA,** *a burly Italian-American judge. Heavy Brooklynese.)*

STANLEY DIANA. September 9, 1940. Stanley A. Diana, duly sworn.

As appears by the records with respect to the above named alien, copies of which are produced and filed herewith:

One. THE ALIENS DID NOT POSSESS IMMIGRATION VISAS.

The aliens admitted that they had never applied for immigration visas, either as immigrants or non-immigrants so that they might come to the United States in a lawful manner.

Two. THE ALIEN ARNOLD SPITZMAN IS ALSO UNDER THE AGE OF SIXTEEN UNACCOMPANIED BY A PARENT OR GUARDIAN.

Three. THE ALIENS SHOULD BE EXCLUDED.

Four. THE ALIENS HAD A FAIR HEARING.

WHEREFORE, said aliens shall be remanded to the custody of the Commissioner of Immigration at Ellis Island, New York Harbor, New York for return to Poland.

Appeal denied.

(The trio is crushed.)

DOLA. Do you think now is a good time to resolve my marriage?

RICHARD. Dola's hilarious. Great timing. But I promised you a triumph. So don't worry.
I worry a lot. Silly things. The planet. My children. The world. The world. The world. They say medication would settle my mind, but I don't want to lose my edge. Maybe hypervigilance runs in the family. Maybe that's why I'm here.
Genka, Fall 1940.

GENKA. Even the strongest person cannot be protected under such horrible circumstances and can break down. And I particularly with my nineteen years have nothing here that can give me some comfort. When it comes to studying there is no possibility. I am grateful that I am working in a store and in this way fill my time up. I hug you, I kiss you, darling uncle.

RICHARD. And yet, her little sister Lusia, same time:

LUSIA. I see thank God everything in bright colors. I feel good and comfortable in the world. I have enough joy in life for this whole highly respected family of ours.

*(**DOLA** appears, injured and traumatized.)*

DOLA. I had an hour-long, very unpleasant interrogation.

JOSEPH. *(Alarmed.) Unpleasant?*

DOLA. Although my conscience is clean I broke down and finally I started to cry and –

(She screams. The adult women comfort her and shield the girls. Was she raped during this interrogation?)

JOSEPH. DOLA.

RICHARD. It could have been anything. But nowhere else do we see the word "unpleasant."
Let's move on.

GENKA. *(Still protected, in her way.)* Dearest Uncle,
Today it is my honor to start this family letter. We are very happy to have permits to stay in Krakow!

JOSEPH. NO!

RICHARD. The Hollanders are among the small minority of Jews allowed to stay in Krakow after the Reich decides that their new territorial capital will be "cleansed."

GENKA. You don't even know how important it is for us not to be forced into some small provincial town without water and electricity.

JOSEPH. Is it really so important? Faucets? Light bulbs? City life?

GENKA. I personally don't have reasons to complain, but I would like all of us to be together again.

> (**KLARA** *wears a religious head scarf for the first time.*)

KLARA. It's only October but it's already cold. I would like to hibernate this winter like the bears do, to see nothing and to hear nothing.
Those who are alive often envy the dead ones now.

MANIA. This Day of Atonement, it is easy to fast. As we have so little. But hard to atone.

DOLA. Harder still to forgive.

KLARA. We must have sinned a lot this year.

> (*She rocks in prayer, shutting down her emotions. This makes her daughters nervous.*)

LUSIA. But now seriously, about my profession! I have all the papers ready. I got my exam which I passed very well! When I have an opportunity I will look for some nice job!

SALO. In connection with deportation actions we will urgently need documents stating that we have already taken some steps in order to be allowed entry into America. I make this request in view of the fact that these documents are very serious and urgent –

JOSEPH. Do you understand I lost my case? I am about to be deported myself. What makes you think I can rescue you?

BERTA. We are going through a time that is not always possible to write about.

JOSEPH. Say more!

BERTA. *(Ordinary "silly mom.")* I wrote you four cards but did not number them. When I write, I think of you, dear child. I forget to number! I am beginning again with Number One.

JOSEPH. How hard is it to remember to number the letters? So I'll know if something is lost!

MANIA. We live as tenants at Mrs. Birnbaum in a tiny room. We eat at Klara's. She is a great housewife. There is always space for anybody to join at the table, a real restaurant. She often has "guests."

KLARA. Within days a German engineer is supposed to move in. We live in two rooms and find it very comfortable. Lusia is very diligent. From nine to three she works at Elwira's and in the afternoon at home, she sews for her customers beautifully.

GENKA. I also work and don't have much time.

MANIA. Lusia is a gift from God, she loves her mother dearly, is very hardworking, helps around the household and sews really well.
If only Genka would like to be half as good as Lusia is, then Klara would be a happy mother.

GENKA. *(Resenting **MANIA**'s criticism.)* I don't know what to write, you know everything anyway. It is really hot here now but nobody goes away!

SALO. We registered ourselves as you instructed with the Consular Division of American Embassy in Berlin; Mania and I are on the waiting list, numbers forty-three thousand seven hundred eleven, and forty-three thousand seven hundred twelve.

MANIA. I eat and drink for my future, because whatever I put into my stomach neither fire nor water will take away from me.

(We see **JOSEPH** *in Jan's New York apartment.)*

BERTA. Dearest Felicja,

How have you organized your housekeeping in your new apartment? I would like so much to be able to see everything, what a joy that would be. When time allows, write me a few lines. I will be very happy to hear good and cheerful things from my only daughter-in-law.

JOSEPH. Will you answer her, darling?

FELICJA. *(Offstage.)* You write and I'll sign.

> *(***JOSEPH*** *reads a letter from* **DOLA** *as she speaks.)*

DOLA. November 5, 1940.

I want to write a letter to Henek.

Actually I already did.

I am sending you the copy of it and I am waiting for your response. Please answer me thoroughly if I should send this letter or rather wait until the end of the war. I wrote it in a provocative manner but I didn't use the word "divorce."

JOSEPH. Divorce?

> *(He listens carefully to* **DOLA.***)*

DOLA. Dear Henek,

You write that we will be happy when the war ends. Forgive me that I am treating this sentence as an empty phrase, since nobody can predict the end of this war. Should I wait for its end? How and with whom?

Our marriage wasn't great. I'll never forget the words you threw in my face: I married you to get out of this little town!

> *(***FELICJA*** *enters, looking swell.)*

FELICJA. We have a situation with the boy, my love.

JOSEPH. Pardon?

FELICJA. He's a bit of a pig.

JOSEPH. He's fourteen years old. That's the age between when a boy needs to wash and when he actually does wash.

FELICJA. My brother is losing patience.

JOSEPH. I swore before the Immigration and Naturalization Court to support and shelter Arnold Spitzman!

RICHARD. But it's hard to fight a woman and her relatives.

DOLA. Henek, if we were a loving couple, I would understand that we are waiting for the end of the war in order to be together again. But you have to admit that our relationship called for separation many times before.

On what should I base the patience for which you so strongly advise? Patience in the name of what? I tell you openly that I don't have this patience and won't force myself to have it.

Please write back, not with the phrases but with the whole truth.

> (*JOSEPH muses on Dola's letter, ignoring* **FELICJA**, *who takes matters into her own hands.*)

FELICJA. Arnie!

> (**ARNOLD** *appears, eating a hot dog.*)

ARNOLD. Yes ma'am?

FELICJA. A nice doctor and his wife uptown have no children, poor things. Here's the address.

> (*She hands him a scrap of paper.*)

And a nickel for the train.

> (**ARNOLD** *exits with a confused glance at* **JOSEPH** *absorbed in his letter.*)

DOLA. Dear Brother,

I am ending my "talk" with you. For a real talk, person-to-person, you never had time, so I am taking revenge on you now.

Please always believe what I write in my letters. I don't add anything and I don't take anything away.

RICHARD. How does Joseph respond?

> (**FELICJA** *perfects her look: hat, lipstick, etc.*)

JOSEPH. *(Furtive.)* Dearest Dola,

What you write to Henek I have wished to say to Felicja as well. I married for the life I expected, a wife for the young man I was.

I of course have disappointed Licja even more severely. She, with her choice of men, selected a fellow with a future, a law graduate, a well-traveled person with a prospering business.

Now I am lucky to find work. Felicja must work. I learn English, I am eager to change. For her the change is not easy.

RICHARD. Or.

JOSEPH. You mustn't, Dola. Marriage is sacred.

RICHARD. Or.

JOSEPH. You marry to take your place in society. And then society ends. And what happens to the marriage?

RICHARD. You may have gathered that Felicja is not my mother.

> (**FELICJA** *exits.*)

DOLA. Dear Mother confiscates your letters and nobody except her can keep them for too long. She puts all of them into a little box organized by dates; they are like good omens for her.

> (**BERTA** *and* **JOSEPH** *may look directly at each other, as if for a moment their bond transcends distance.*)

BERTA. You say you find work.

JOSEPH. You say you eat plenty.

BERTA. You say you left Jan Schreiber's.

JOSEPH. You say the family stays safe.

BERTA. You say you and Felicja are expecting good news.

JOSEPH. Who is Klara's German guest?

BERTA. What kind of work do you do?

JOSEPH. How did Mania break her hand?

BERTA. Who is the boy Arnold Spitzman and what is he like in your home?

JOSEPH & BERTA. I flip through your letters like a recipe. Guessing at the secret ingredients.

> *(In Krakow, the* **FAMILY** *toasts. Sudden full joy!)*

SALO. *Viva Nicaragua!*

ALL. *Viva Nicaragua!*

DOLA. Many special thanks for the papers you sent us! You cannot imagine with what great joy we welcomed them.

MANIA. Salo carries these papers with him all the time, just like a talisman!

SALO. *Viva Nicaragua!*

GENKA. How to thank you for such a wonderful present like a trip to Nicaragua? Nicaragua – how wonderful it sounds!

LUSIA. I got so enthusiastic that I decided to become a journalist over there. What do you think of that?

MANIA. The girls tried to locate the place on the map! We have been consulting the dictionary to learn about the language and the people.

ALL. Viva Nicaragua!

GENKA. These papers fell like stars from the sky! We simply lost our heads out of joy! Aunt Dola makes us call her "señora" and Dad plans the whole future for himself. He wants to become a newspaper delivery man over there!

KLARA. Lusia will be a journalist, and Dawid will deliver the papers.

LUSIA. I would like to know something more specific about the land of our future. Is it a land that flows with milk and honey? What language do they speak there?

ALL. Nicaragua!

RICHARD. We don't know how Dad got those papers for Nicaragua. Was he some kind of magician?

ALL. Nicaragua!

BERTA. It is not possible to write family letters because now all letters must be written by only one hand. I wanted to write you in my own handwriting.
(Whisper.) Nicaragua!

RICHARD. Oh, Nicaragua.

> *(Beat.)*

How miraculous that Joseph got them so close.

> *(In Krakow, joy thuds to a close. Only* **JOSEPH** *stays hopeful.)*

DOLA. You gave us a travel route. Well it's now forbidden to leave the Reich.

MANIA. I know that you moved earth and heaven for us so we could leave for Nicaragua. But it's beyond your power.

SALO. *(Overcome.)* Please forgive me that I am so dry today. My heart is so full, as if a belt of steel were tied around it. It is ready to burst.

JOSEPH. Hold on to the documents for Nicaragua. They are validated by the German consulate. If circumstances change, they could be enough.

DOLA. Today on the street an unknown woman told me that her brother was at Henek's funeral. My husband died in December.

BERTA. I hope everything is all right with you two. For us it is Tisha B'Av *[TISH-uh BUHV]*.

RICHARD. The Jewish day of mourning all catastrophes. Very clever of Berta to write the Hebrew phrase in her educated Hapsburg German script. Got through uncensored.

DOLA. Among friends and acquaintances, tragic trips into the unknown have already started.

KLARA. May God help us to spend the winter together here.

BERTA. I know that it may be wrong for me to write you such a thing, but a drowning person grabs at a straw to save himself. My heart is full, my eyes fill with tears. We are in front of water.

JOSEPH. Don't wait for me to solve this. Try to move now.

You all speak Polish, and can blend in with Poles, which most Jews cannot. You are in an excellent position to split up and live as Catholics. Move. Now.

BERTA. *(Whispers.)* May the lucky star never leave you. My precious, my love, my only son, my treasure. May you shine for us all.

KRAKOW FAMILY. May you shine for us all.

JOSEPH. Letters I don't write but send food instead:

The letter about the divorce.

The letter about the rats.

The letter where we lose the immigration appeal.

The letter where I break my promise to the boy and Arnold Spitzman becomes a foster child after all.

The letter where they laugh at my English.

The letter where a boss withholds my pay.

The letter where I sleep on daybeds, and for one night in Grand Central Station.

The letter where I skip dinner for a week to send you chocolate.

The letter stating the cost of those Nicaragua papers.

The letter where I enlist in the U.S. Army, my only chance for citizenship.

The letter where I learn that because I speak German, I must serve in Germany.

And recalling these letters I did not write from the reasonably safe streets of New York City, I must wonder: my sisters, Dear Mother, girls, and brothers-in-law: what are the letters you did not write?

MANIA. There are things you can experience but cannot describe.

We will write you about what happens next: we will either leave or move to the Jewish quarter in Podgórze.

RICHARD. Phase Three: The Krakow Ghetto.

> *(By now the* **FAMILY** *is ragged. But before we descend, a bright note:)*

DOLA. *(Warm, new tone.)* My dear brother,
You will be very surprised at the content of this letter.

JOSEPH. Where are you, Dola? Did you escape somehow?

DOLA. I want to inform you that on Tuesday, March 18 I will marry a man I have known for eighteen months now.

JOSEPH. *What?*

RICHARD. Heh heh, not what you were expecting, eh? *Love finds a way!*

DOLA. I met him at the beginning of the war; he was always a source of tremendous support for me in the most difficult moments. I am not going to list for you all his good sides (he has bad ones as well) because you may think that I am regressing back to my teenage years. His name is Munio. Munio Blaustein.

> *(Normal family gossip:)*

BERTA. My dear child if you receive a letter from Dola, do not be surprised that she has taken such a step. As her mother I encouraged her. She was a thorn in the side.

KLARA. I was not for Dola getting married now.

MANIA. I agree with Dear Mother and disagree with Klara. It's easy to say for Klara because she has a husband and children. Dola didn't have anybody.

DOLA. My dearest brother, life surprises us sometimes in a strange way. Maybe I will finally taste some happiness as well.

RICHARD. By this point in 1941, the Jews who were allowed to remain in Krakow moved to the Ghetto, which was established not in the Jewish quarter as expected, but in Podgórze, an ugly, shabby part of town. Near the railroad tracks.

(A room in the crowded, ramshackle Krakow Ghetto.)

LUSIA. In which spring will we see each other again? Will I still be in my teens?

> *(**GENKA** is a spirited, generous young woman now, grown from the moody teen. Not complaining.)*

GENKA. I am afraid of winter because my fingers and toes are frostbitten and I don't have mittens or snow shoes. But somehow I have to survive.

The most important thing is not to give up, right?

We are pleased in our apartment. We have full comfort here although it is furnished very poorly, almost funny. Some old junk that keeps shaking in all directions. But we have a beautiful light room with two windows.

JOSEPH. "A" room. For how many of you?

GENKA. The letters from you Dear Uncle are always the best gift and a big attraction. We all are really touched that you remember us.

JOSEPH. That I *remember* you?

GENKA & JOSEPH. You are my hope for the future.

GENKA. I didn't change much outside but inside I feel a quarter-century older. I often regret that I didn't leave with you, but maybe it is better this way, I would only be a burden to you.

What's new in your life? I am curious what you are doing in this moment when I am typing this letter to you on our old Erica. I would give so much to know.

I believe that everything is possible, things are just more or less probable.

> *(**JOSEPH** puts down the letter. He can't take it anymore.)*

BERTA. Write more details about yourselves, not simply about work but just private things. I have not had a letter from you for a long time and wish very much for one. It cannot be as long as it seems to me, since every day lasts a year.

RICHARD. *Every Day Lasts a Year.*

> *(He holds up his book, staying on-message.)*

> *(In the Krakow Ghetto, the* **FAMILY** *delights in a package. Brisk, overlapping, upbeat:)*

KLARA. On your birthday we received a package from Lisbon containing coffee, tea, sugar, soap, / and three boxes of tinned food.

MANIA. We got seven small packages, all from Portugal, / and paid for in Lisbon.

BERTA. We also received a notification from Warsaw that there is condensed / milk waiting for us!

GENKA & LUSIA. A separate thank you for the / powdered chocolate.

SALO. When will we be able to pay you back?

DOLA. I finally feel that somebody takes care of me.

BERTA. What else can I write to you?

KRAKOW FAMILY. *(Staggered unison.)* **What else can I write to you?**

> *(The* **FAMILY** *vanishes. It's terrifying.)*

RICHARD. The last letter comes from Dola's brother-in-law in Switzerland almost two years later, December 5, 1943.

> *(He reads.)*

"Dear Mr. Hollander,

Yesterday I received a check for fifty dollars that you sent from the bank. In this moment I cannot send it to Dola. But I will hold it for her.

Unfortunately I have to inform you that your Dear Mother died peacefully and without pain on August 28, 1942. It is God's will and we humans cannot help it."

Sure this note is sad, but consider the context.

> *(Violin music.* Sentimental.* **RICHARD** *is
> moved, but in his comfort zone.)*

Berta Hollander, the matriarch, who kept her family together with fierce love, dies peacefully in a time of war.

Although Joseph surely grieved, what a comfort. To know the mother he admired and loved so dearly died with her dignity. I picture Mania holding her hand, as Genka sings a tune.

And Joseph triumphed! He stayed in America and began a new family.

We may weep, it's only natural. But we must always, always celebrate life. And when a treasure like this *(The book, his message.)* passes from one generation to the next, despite the dark forces of history, we celebrate with all our might!

Thank you for coming tonight, to witness a hero. To approach the mystery. To deepen our humanity. Because it's the tough times that teach us who us are.

Now go home and hug your families. Study hard. Brush your teeth. Good night and God bless.

> **(CRAIG** *enters, carrying a small, battered
> briefcase. Nerdy manic. Hyper contemporary.)*

CRAIG. *That* was your talk?

> *(This was not the plan.)*

RICHARD. My middle child, Craig Hollander. Grad student. Studies slave narratives. Happy guy.

CRAIG. Tell me you don't do this every night.

RICHARD. The tree flourishes.

CRAIG. It's the tough times that teach us who we are? Seriously?

---

*A license to produce *The Book of Joseph* does not include a performance license for any third-party or copyrighted music. Licensees should create an original composition or use music in the public domain. For further information, please see Music Use Note on page 3.

RICHARD. I told the truth.

CRAIG. Like the part about your grandma dying peacefully? By 1942, she could have starved to death, she could have been shot on the street. Elderly people were massacred in groups to save bullets –

RICHARD. The letter said, peacefully and without pain.

CRAIG. The letters lied!

(To audience.) After the accident –

RICHARD. Thank you for attending my book talk!

CRAIG. He didn't tell you about the accident. He didn't tell you about this *briefcase*.

RICHARD. Why would you carry that old –

CRAIG. He didn't mention that he let these scraps sit fifteen years because he was so scared of what they might say.

RICHARD. This is a poignant but hopeful ending!

CRAIG. Nope. You're not done.

(To audience.) Do what you people need to do. We'll see you here in fifteen.

(Lights start to fade.)

RICHARD. The rest will be brief!

CRAIG. I can't promise that.

RICHARD. Thirty minutes.

CRAIG. Ish.

RICHARD. Remember what Joseph went through to get that coffee and chocolate to his family? Lucky you can just buy it in the lobby!

(As lights fade:)

RICHARD. And the book! About twenty bucks!

CRAIG. Dad stop hawking your book, it's unseemly.

RICHARD. The proceeds go to charity.

CRAIG. Oh that's different.

RICHARD. I have a lot of faults but greed isn't one.

CRAIG. Let the people take their break.

RICHARD. Where did I park?

ACT TWO

(A fresh aura of wartime romance. New Jersey, 1944. **VITA FISCHMAN** *rides a train. She's nicely dressed.* **JOSEPH**, *in an American Army uniform, sits beside her reading a book of Polish poetry.* **VITA**, *despite being well-bred, is curious.)*

VITA. Excuse me. What are you reading?

JOSEPH. *(Lighter Polish accent.)* It's poetry.

> *(The poem is* In Raspberry Bushes *by Bolesław Leśmian.)*

*W malinowym chruśniaku, przed ciekawych wzrokiem
Zapodziani po głowy, przez długie godziny.*

VITA. Goodness.

JOSEPH. You studied poetry?

VITA. I studied art. I drew Popeye and Betty Boop for Fleisher Studios in Florida.

JOSEPH. Wonderful. Like Mickey and Minnie Mouse?

VITA. Mr. Disney won't let girls draw. Only fill in the lines.

JOSEPH. How foolish.

VITA. I thought so. Now I work for the army. I illustrate the insides of captured Kraut electronics.

JOSEPH. Wowie.

VITA. I'm just doing my part.

JOSEPH. I was in Florida.

VITA. Beautiful area.

JOSEPH. I was having a divorce.

VITA. Oh.

JOSEPH. You wear a diamond.

VITA. I'm engaged to a doctor.

JOSEPH. May he heal the heart.

VITA. From what wound?

>   *(Beat.)*

JOSEPH. Forgive me. I know too many immigrants. Of course your heart is intact.

>   *(They ride.)*

VITA. Would you...

JOSEPH. Yes?

VITA. Would you read another line?

JOSEPH. For you? A thousand lines.
>   *Zrywaliśmy przybyłe tej nocy maliny.*
>   *Palce miałaś na oślep skrwawione ich sokiem.*

VITA. Are you European?

JOSEPH. Yes. European. Dr. Josef Hollander. But a doctor only of the law, I'm afraid.

VITA. A lawyer.

JOSEPH. In Europe. Here I'm a common enlisted boy. A dozen of me on every corner.

VITA. I doubt that.

JOSEPH. Perhaps only on the more populated corners.

VITA. Vita Fischman.

JOSEPH. Pretty name. Vita. The life.

VITA. That's what they say.

JOSEPH. He is a lucky doctor.

VITA. I feel strange.

JOSEPH. Perhaps the motion –

VITA. *(The poem.)* What does it mean?

JOSEPH. In the raspberry bush...you and I, away from the... curious. Lost up to our heads, for hours.

>   *(**VITA**'s thoughts:)*

VITA. We ride the 7:40 to Red Bank, he reads the poem, and suddenly we are riding our lives. I am thirty he is forty, I am fifty he is sixty, I am seventy, he is eighty – I'm driving! I love to drive. The road becomes our road.

(She drives. The sudden squeal of brakes. She presents **JOSEPH** *to her parents.)*

Mother! Daddy! The wedding is off! I met a divorced Polish immigrant!

*(***RICHARD*** *narrates, in his element again.* **CRAIG** *looks on impatiently.* **JOSEPH** *and* **VITA** *stay visible. Sepia, romantic.)*

RICHARD. They married in City Hall. But he promised her parents a Jewish wedding after the war. He kept the promise and so for forty years my very courtly father celebrated not one but two anniversaries. So romantic.

CRAIG. What are you doing, Dad?

RICHARD. You wanted more of the story.

CRAIG. Not about them. About you.

RICHARD. But Papa was a hero and I'm just a person.

CRAIG. I know. You're more relatable.

(To audience.) Ask him how he found the letters.

RICHARD. The first rule of journalism: You are Not the Story.

CRAIG. That's a very twentieth-century rule.

RICHARD. *(To audience.)* After City Hall, Joseph and Vita spend one night at the St. Regis Hotel. You wanna see the bill?

CRAIG. Uh, no they don't.

RICHARD. Dad reports for basic training the next day.

JOSEPH. March 3, 1945.

My Darlink-Wife,

Today is thirteen months since the lucky moment when I met you. I don't like to be sentimental, but I have this wonderful feeling to have someone in the world so near to me. Someone about whom I can think, plan and be happy. Yes, darlink, I am happy and hope and pray to make you happy.

Darlink – (at least you don't hear my bad pronunciation of the "g") I hold you tight and kiss your little nose.

Always yours, Joe.

RICHARD. A storybook romance.

CRAIG. Did you notice my dad talks in a kind of stock footage? Like every experience is prepackaged into a neat box of message.

RICHARD. Whatsa matter with a message?

VITA. Dear Husband,

The salutation appears austere, but darling it feels warm and good to say "dear husband." A thousand dreams and hopes are within that word which is woman's whole existence.

CRAIG. Kinda sexist.

JOSEPH. Dearest Wife,

The whole crowd called, "This man hit the jackpot" when the mail-call handed over to me a pack of nineteen letters from you last night. "Jackpot" is not the right name for it. If I can use a common expression I would say – I broke the bank in Monte Carlo.

RICHARD. Dad and I share a sense of humor, but he's funny.

JOSEPH. The first thing what I did, I took out a pass for the evening and went alone to the nearby forest, lied down on the ground, read your letters and read them over and over again until it was dark. Later I was talking to you and I was feeling you with all my five senses.

CRAIG. Sassy.

RICHARD. Grow up.

JOSEPH. All those letters were your first letters to me. Letters written by a newlywed girl with love to her husband. I needed those letters. They warmed up my heart, gave me energy to go through this waiting period with confidence of our happiness to the end of our days. If it will happen that I will not have anything to leave to our children, I will give them those first letters. They contain the purest love and faith and what can be bigger and more desired for a human being?

I am sure that you will have some troubles understanding my letters, but I will not write any drafts first. I will wrote what I think even with mistakes. The only thing I am sure off – I don't make any mistakes in my mind. With love, Joe.

VITA. Never make excuses about being sentimental – because I fell in love with and married a sentimental pick-up – don't let me find out too late that you are devoid of sentiment! Yes, darling I am near to you – very, very near.

Always always write as you feel, and forget whether it's in English or Hindustan – I'll understand.

CRAIG. That's your happy ending? They write love letters and birth you.

RICHARD. *(To audience.)* Walking around Krakow –

CRAIG. *(Provocative.)* When did you go to Poland, Dad?

RICHARD. Walking around Krakow, I had a new feeling: "You know what Nazis? I'm here and you're not. I got three kids. They're going on in this world, and you know. I'm not defeated." Remember that.

CRAIG. Then we *are* the story.

RICHARD. *(To audience.)* Thank you for your purchases past and future. I'll say goodnight now.

CRAIG. *(To audience.)* Okay, you probably figured out that anywhere dead people spoke directly to each other, that was fiction.

RICHARD. Fiction? This is a documentary work! The National Archives has a four-hundred-page file on my father. His letter to Eleanor Roosevelt.

CRAIG. That part was real.

RICHARD. And *every word* the family wrote to Joseph is real.

CRAIG. Yes. You've been extremely faithful not to add anything to the letters.

RICHARD. All the court documents. Stanley Diana, the immigration hearing, all of it.

CRAIG. Yes.

RICHARD. This matters to people, I want to be very clear here. I'm not making things up.

CRAIG. Every word in every official document, and in every letter from the family to Joseph is authentic.

RICHARD. A true story! Nothing added! Plenty was removed, so I do recommend you / buy the –

CRAIG. But obviously anything *Joseph* wrote to *Poland*? Let's use the real tough scrutiny of common sense. Joseph kept his family's letters safely numbered, in New York.

RICHARD. Yes, I did my best to create a real picture in your mind of –

CRAIG. Berta kept Joseph's letters safely numbered, *in the Krakow Ghetto* which was liquidated in 1942.

So whoops, no artifacts.

RICHARD. My parents' love letters are real.

CRAIG. True. But that vague party at the beginning? Eleven visas to Lisbon? Who frickin' knows?

RICHARD. What's your point?

CRAIG. You answered questions that we can't answer. You got sentimental instead of curious. Why didn't Joseph and Felicja raise Arnold Spitzman? When and why did they get divorced? How did they travel to Florida when they had no legal papers in the U.S.? No one knows. It's gone.

RICHARD. So much survived.

CRAIG. Until the accident, my dad didn't even know he *had* relatives in Poland.

Joseph kept it quiet. Richard followed suit. That's the tradition. Silence.

RICHARD. The Hollanders focus on the positive. Most of us. My son Craig, a bright child who could have done anything, hopes to be a professor of slave trade correspondence.

CRAIG. Uh, "professor of slave trade correspondence" isn't really a thing.

RICHARD. I know that. Do you know that?

CRAIG. Since you brought it up, Dad, the slaver letters are a great example. You can't just fill in the blanks. It's ahistoric and it's wrong.

Tell them how this started.

RICHARD. Krakow, 1939.

CRAIG. Baltimore, 1986.

(He holds up the briefcase.)

RICHARD. That belongs in my study.

CRAIG. This is what we have. This, and you. And one more thing, if you want to see.

RICHARD. Every morning my mother read the newspaper first, with her art scissors. She removed any mention of the war.

CRAIG. That's codependent.

RICHARD. That was love.

CRAIG. Why didn't you ask questions?

RICHARD. You know what I learned from my father that you little no offense shits have the luxury of ignoring? To be happy you look at what is in *front of you.* My dad had a lot. He also lost a lot. But that is not where he looked, do you understand?

CRAIG. If he'd lived longer I would have gotten the whole story out of him.

RICHARD. I have no doubt. You spare no one.

CRAIG. You were the journalist.

RICHARD. I was not ruthless. I see people, not evidence.

CRAIG. Do you Dad? Do you see people? Or do you just see your footage?

(To audience.) Just five years after Joseph escaped Europe, he returned as an American GI at the end of the war. Yes, he was in love with his wife. But he did not, in fact, forget.

JOSEPH. Vita, my darling,

This big sign greeted us when we crossed the Dutch/ German borderline two days ago: "You are entering *Germany.* Be always on your guard. Don't fraternize."

With this sign, something happened to me.

(A vengeful tone we have not heard.) For you and everyone with whom you will talk I like to state – after traveling for three days on German soil and deep inside of that country – **they got what they asked for.**

RICHARD. *(To audience.)* This tone is atypical.

JOSEPH. We drove for hours seeing only ruins of buildings. The destruction was so complete that from the mountains of debris we could never say whether it was before a house, a factory, or a church. A wonderful scenery for a Wagnerian play. **Let them play now!**

RICHARD. My father was a kind and gentle man.

JOSEPH. Believe me Vita, I am not a hard-boiled egg, and this type of human annihilation would always touch me very deeply, but not now and not against German men and women. When I see them pushing on the roads little carriages with their belongings I am not sorry for them at all. It exists an expression, "the revenge is sweet," yes, very sweet. And I feel it, even if I could not yet personally do my share.

(He sees **VITA**. *He softens and opens.)*

In the last four days since I left Belgium, I'm freezing by day and night. It's cold like December in Siberia, rainy like January in Egypt, foggy like February in London, and windy like on the Atlantic Avenue subway station where I was waiting for the train to take me to Grant Avenue. Wonderful train! I wish I could stay there now and be fully exposed to this pleasant wind. It would be for me a real May with all its beauty.

(A harsh squeal of brakes. **RICHARD** *flinches.)*

RICHARD. *(Pleading.)* Can we leave it here? Please?

(To audience.) Thank you that's it safe home.

CRAIG. Do you want to go home? I'll take you home.

RICHARD. I'm fine.

CRAIG. *(To audience.)* Thanks for coming.

(To **RICHARD**.*)* Here we go. I'm right here. We're home.

> *(Elements of a realistic domestic space emerge, as if Craig's concern has magically brought Richard home. There is no longer a book talk. Father and son alone for the first time.* **CRAIG** *speaks tenderly.)*

Dad. Would you tell me about the accident?

(**RICHARD** *is unguarded now, no showman. Just seeing the events, quietly.*)

RICHARD. I am thirty-eight years old. My children are six, four, and one. We are in evening mode: divide and conquer. I play checkers with you and Hillary; Ellen puts Baby Brett to sleep.

The phone rings. Maybe Mom saying they've arrived. It was a warm night. They were headed home to Westchester from Florida. Visiting your great-grandma. My father. My mother. The phone.

CRAIG. Mom screamed like. Like I never heard a person scream. Like I wouldn't know a person could scream.

RICHARD. Ellen had a fuller reaction. In that moment. She absorbed something. In that moment.

I start asking questions. I'm a reporter so I go into reporter mode. "What is your badge number officer? I need to get a pencil. I need to take this down."

I go to the bedroom. I speak on the extension. I sit on the side of the bed, taking notes. Ellen is screaming; she's calling her mother. The kids are screaming.

CRAIG. Mom's a pretty cool customer, generally.

RICHARD. I sit down. Like this.

(*With effort, he sits all the way down on the ground, legs in front of him, his back against a piece of furniture. Silence.*)

I just sit down. Like this. I sit.

(**CRAIG** *sits down, copying* **RICHARD***'s position, back against furniture, legs in front, but more comfortably, as a younger man sits.*)

I mean, I didn't speak, I didn't cry, I sat there. I mean, like.

Like coma – like catatonic state.

(*The two men sit a while, in the exact same position.* **RICHARD** *breaks into an anecdote, the stock footage.*)

RICHARD. It's like my father, you know in New York, in Manhattan, often people come to you and they're selling you hot watches and things. Well one time my father's alone in the middle of daylight walking through Bryant Park, to his office, he had a travel office on Forty-sixth Street, he's drifting in his thoughts, a guy comes up to him, puts a handgun in the middle of his stomach, *clearly robbing him*, and my father thinks oh a gun, he's trying to sell me a gun, and he just keeps walking. Across the park. Well he got to the other side of the park and suddenly the adrenaline surged and he thought, oh my god, I just ignored a guy robbing me at gunpoint.

It's like the robber's probably expecting any response: struggling, throwing the wallet, fighting back, screaming. No robber expects to be ignored. Dad just said, "I'm not interested," and kept walking.

You never know what your response is going to be. Your life is turned upside down in one second.

CRAIG. Dad?

RICHARD. Son?

CRAIG. When did you find the briefcase?

> (**RICHARD** *is subdued again, experiencing, not storytelling.*)

RICHARD. I went to their home. Everything was – food in the refrigerator, window cracked for air. They were coming back.

CRAIG. Did you find it that day?

RICHARD. The – *what*? No. I was planning a funeral.

CRAIG. What did I do wrong at the funeral?

RICHARD. You did nothing wrong. You were four years old.

CRAIG. I remember being punished.

RICHARD. You can't wrap your mind around death when you're a little kid.

CRAIG. Mom gave me a choice between two different punishments, and the one I chose, she chose the opposite one.

RICHARD. That right?

CRAIG. It was very clever. I remember being like, oh is that how we're going to play this one?

RICHARD. Yup.

CRAIG. It was probably like a week without television or a week without candy.

RICHARD. Yup.

CRAIG. Yup what?

RICHARD. *(Foggy.)* What?

> *(Beat.)*

CRAIG. How exactly did they die?

RICHARD. To go at eighty, instantly, next to the love of your life. I'll take it. Eighty-five would be better.

CRAIG. Did you identify their bodies?

RICHARD. Yes.

CRAIG. Was there impact? Pressure to the head? To organs? Broken glass?

RICHARD. They always wore safety belts.

CRAIG. I know.

RICHARD. For a European man. To learn to wear a safety belt... Your papa loved life. He loved us. He loved my mother like a prince in a story. He let her drive.

CRAIG. I'd like to be able to picture it.

RICHARD. *Why?*

CRAIG. My advisor says every great historian is communing with the dead.

RICHARD. Jesus.

CRAIG. Please go on.

RICHARD. Your mom and I go to pack up the house. It's a you know classic 1950s split-level. In the upstairs bedroom there's a closet three feet off the ground, a crawl space. Not even a full attic.
It's pretty dark in there.
I look to my right and there is a stand-alone briefcase, not an expensive briefcase, just an old thing, and I open it up.

(He opens the briefcase. We hear bits and pieces of the family's letters in Polish. A whispered cacophony.)

RICHARD. In rubber bands all the stuff was there, all these letters. I saw the swastikas, and I saw a couple hundred letters, numbered and very neatly stacked. Addressed to my dad. Obviously I didn't know what was in them. I mean Polish, you can't get a clue.

CRAIG. Did you think it might hold something incriminating?

RICHARD. Incriminating? Yes. I lost my parents. I lost my mother. I lost my father.

I thought I could lose – I knew my father as a good man.

(Voices switch to German.)

You see the swastikas; you know he survived the war. You don't want to ask.

CRAIG. *You* don't want to ask.

RICHARD. I shut the case.

(He does. Voices stop.)

In that moment, with three little rugrat adorable kids and two great jobs and so much sorrow, I thought: no good can come of this. I told myself –

*(**CRAIG** following **RICHARD**; this is something **RICHARD** says all the time:)*

RICHARD & CRAIG. I'm dealing with a lot now. I just can't deal, I just can't – deal with one more thing –

RICHARD. – Is what I said to myself. You owe it to your children to get back in the saddle. Kids are entitled to a life without detours, no interruptions. You have like a fiduciary duty to do the playdates and the swimming and the fucking carpools. **Kids have to think you're happy.**

CRAIG. I never thought you were happy.

RICHARD. My mistake. One of many. If I live long enough I'm sure you'll document the rest.

CRAIG. Did you think Papa was happy?

RICHARD. **He was happy!** He loved my mother! He loved to travel! He loved me! It wasn't an act! You remember him, don't you?

CRAIG. Sure.

RICHARD. **He was a happy goddamn person!**
    Anyway, I shut the case.

CRAIG. "The moment I found these letters, I vowed to shine a light on this family"?

RICHARD. Maybe not that exact moment.

CRAIG. How long did you wait, Dad?

VOICES OF KRAKOW FAMILY. *(Accusatory.)* 1986.
    1987.
    1988.
    1989.

CRAIG. And then?

VOICES OF KRAKOW FAMILY. 1990.
    1991.
    1992.
    1993.
    1994.

CRAIG. And then?

VOICES OF KRAKOW FAMILY. 1995.
    1996.
    1997.
    1998.
    1999.

RICHARD. In 1999 you begged me to get them translated. For a high school history project.

CRAIG. You said no.

VOICES OF KRAKOW FAMILY. 2000.
    2001.
    2002.

CRAIG. And then?

VOICES OF KRAKOW FAMILY. 2003.

2004.

RICHARD. 2004. I am fifty-five years old. My children are twenty-three, twenty-one, and eighteen. I hire a woman to translate the letters. A Polish Catholic, a young professor at American University. I walk into her home a week later and she's sobbing. The translator is sobbing. She's not even Jewish. She tells me: You don't know what you have here. You don't know what you had.

By then everyone was dead.

CRAIG. Well yeah –

RICHARD. I mean the *survivors* were dead.

I found the letters in 1986. Around that time, there was great interest in survivors' stories. Spielberg did video recordings. He released *Schindler's List* in 1993, it takes place in the Krakow Ghetto. Survivors gathered for the premiere, people who knew my family. They could have told me something. They were alive. Also, Mania mentions at one point, "Greetings from the pharmacist Pankiewicz."

Tadeusz Pankiewicz wrote a book about the Krakow Ghetto. He lived until 1999. He would have remembered my family. I could have found him.

The Holocaust was memory, and when I wasn't looking it turned into history.

You want to do this? You want the list of what I could have learned between 1986 and 2004 if I had not been so afraid to look? You want my coulda shoulda list? It's long.

CRAIG. Coulda, shoulda, and woulda went fishing, and the boat sank.

RICHARD. That's my joke.

CRAIG. You really want to claim it?

RICHARD. My father invited me to Poland.

CRAIG. That's the first thing you told me that I didn't already know.

RICHARD. Maybe he knew it was his last chance, to see his homeland. I think he wanted to do several things. He wanted to retrieve his diploma from university. He wanted to see his parents' graves. He asked me; he said son, would you like to come with?

CRAIG. *(Softly.)* Would you like to come with?

RICHARD. I really didn't want to go, I didn't want to go, I was so busy with –

I didn't want to see him suffer. That was the only time he really said, he wanted to share this with me. I said no thank you. He did not ask again.

That's grown-up life, Craig.

CRAIG. Oh.

RICHARD. I shoulda gone on that trip. And the boat sank.

CRAIG. You didn't want to see him suffer.

RICHARD. *I* didn't want to suffer. I was a coward.

CRAIG. That's oversimplifying.

RICHARD. You're a real comfort, you know that, kid?

CRAIG. If I can be blunt –

RICHARD. For a change.

CRAIG. Hil's worried.

RICHARD. What the hell is this?

CRAIG. She thinks you're like, frozen.

RICHARD. When does your sister have time to gossip about me on the phone?

CRAIG. Text. Hillary theorizes that maybe you couldn't feel. At the time. With us so little and you and Mom working so hard. But that now there's less distraction. And her theory is that maybe you. You know. Are sad.

RICHARD. My daughter theorizes by text that I am sad.

CRAIG. Well she used a different word.

RICHARD. Is this an intervention?

CRAIG. No, if it were an intervention everyone would take the day off. She just mentioned / it –

RICHARD. The D word?

CRAIG. Which D word do / you mean?

RICHARD. Depression.

CRAIG. Damage.

RICHARD. Oh for Chrissakes –

CRAIG. That's not judgmental, Dad. You should see these slave trade letters from men who *perpetrated* but also / *witnessed* –

RICHARD. WHY ARE YOU STUDYING SLAVE TRADE LETTERS?

CRAIG. WHY DO YOU THINK?!

> (*Beat.* **CRAIG** *was dead serious, but* **RICHARD** *blows it off.*)

RICHARD. Great I'm to blame for that too when you can't get a job. "White male seeks professorship of African American Studies." What were you thinking?

CRAIG. I followed my passion.

RICHARD. Rookie move.

CRAIG. Forget I came.

> (*He turns to leave with the briefcase.*)

RICH. You tried to jump into their graves.

CRAIG. What?

RICHARD. That's why you got punished. You were four, you lost your granny and papa; we must have said they were in the boxes. Normal people run from the pain, you run towards it.

CRAIG. To be with them?

RICHARD. I don't know.

CRAIG. I tried to jump in their *graves*?

RICHARD. It was upsetting.

CRAIG. And Mom took away my *TV*?

RICHARD. Could have been candy.

CRAIG. What kind of parenting is *that*?

RICHARD. You will have a child one day, I hope. And you will notice: they arrive without instructions.
This one gets me.

(He shows **CRAIG** *a letter.)*

JOSEPH. Vita, my sweetheart, explaining why I don't write about war: a couple weeks ago I wrote a long letter on this subject, but I tore the letter and did not send it.

CRAIG. Why?

JOSEPH. I will rather restrict myself to more personal matters.

Your lover, Joe.

(Agitated, hopeful.) P.S. I finished this letter and making my bed I found under the sleeping bag a letter from a Miss Blaustein from Paris.

MISS BLAUSTEIN. I am the sister of Munio Blaustein who married your sister Dola. I have something to tell you about your family.

JOSEPH. The first thing tomorrow morning (it's midnight now) I will try to get a two-days pass to go to Paris. I will have to hitchhike. Most probably it will take me around ten hours each way, but I must go. In case you will not get letters for two days you will know why.

(We see **MISS BLAUSTEIN** *in the rooming house. She may wear men's clothing.)*

When I entered her shabby little room in this third-class rooming house the first thing poor Miss Blaustein did, she started to cry. Later she showed the symptoms of the well-known refugee disease: she wanted by any means to proof to me who she was before the war, how rich she was and started to dig out documents.

MISS BLAUSTEIN. This was my home. This was my bank statement. Our tax return.

JOSEPH. My efforts to stop all this exhibition didn't help.

MISS BLAUSTEIN. A receipt for my fur.

JOSEPH. And here again in tears this unhappy lady told me –

MISS BLAUSTEIN. I hid three years in cellars, in Paris. Do you want to know how I survived?

JOSEPH. It was gruesome to listen to this. It's remarkable how strong is in a person the will to live, when in her age she is ready to fight and go through all this misery just to save the naked life.

MISS BLAUSTEIN. But! I was in a continuous correspondence with my brother Munio and your sister Dola until July 1944. Here are the last three cards she wrote.

JOSEPH. 1944!

MISS BLAUSTEIN. Every one is just a few words, as a sign they are alive. Those cards were mailed to your other sister –

JOSEPH. Klara!

MISS BLAUSTEIN. Take them.

> (**JOSEPH** *takes the cards, like living things.*)

JOSEPH. To the last card, dated July 3, 1944, less than *one year ago*, Klara added *in her own writing*:

KLARA. *(Good news.)* We are leaving unexpectedly with a transport for exchange. We will send to you our new address after our arrival.

JOSEPH. It is clear to me that they left Krakow, but neither I know where they have been shipped nor who was shipped. My sister wrote "we." Was it she with her husband and children or under "we" she meant also my oldest sister Mania with her husband?

> (*He rereads, filled with hope.*)

KLARA & JOSEPH. We are leaving unexpectedly with a transport for exchange.

JOSEPH. They all had the same documents for Nicaragua which I mailed to them in 1940! Only on basis of this papers could be used by the German authorities the word "exchange" which my sister repeated in her last note. *If* she would write, "We are leaving with a transport," and she would not mention the word "for exchange," I would think that it was one of those dreadful transports.

Can I have hope to see them yet alive?

I traveled from one camp to another without any result until after ten p.m. and drove back through the night. I will like to spare you, and therefore I will not write about all what I learned and saw.

VITA. We are wondering whether you were part of the occupation forces that occupied Berlin on July 4. It's nice to think that you would be with them – an almost personal triumph for you.

JOSEPH. I broke up a piece of marble from the pedestal on which Hitler stood and a piece of Hitler's marble desk on which he signed to law treaties and agreements he never kept, and so many murder decrees he fulfilled to the last letter.

I am using every opportunity to talk to Poles in the camps of displaced persons (there are over three million Poles in Germany) asking for someone from Krakow in the hope that he may know someone from my family.

VITA. The news you have been looking for all these years might be closer now. Please darling, should it be bad news, take it! And know that you have me to come home to, in another world.

JOSEPH. Today one woman confirmed that *just last year* two transports each of 150 persons with the best documents have been sent from the camp Belsen to an unknown destination for exchange with German citizens. My sister and her family were in one of those transports!

This woman assures me that many people from Poland are alive and scattered throughout the world and pretty soon we'll hear from them! I hope she's right!

Dearest, I am waiting to spend some of the brightest and most stimulating years of my life with you. Now our happiness will be so much bigger, because we know we belong to each other.

No more separate riding on trains and buses.

JOSEPH & VITA. Together to our home, however and whatever it will be.

> (**JOSEPH** *and* **VITA** *approach each other, end of the war. American music.* *They ride together.* **VITA** *drives.*)

KRAKOW FAMILY VOICES. 1945. 1950. 1955. 1960. 1965. 1970. 1975. 1980. 1985.

RICHARD. Forty fairytale years.

> (*Shock on* **VITA***'s face. Brakes squeal, now the full sound of a crash.* **RICHARD** *flinches terribly.* **RICHARD** *and* **CRAIG** *are alone again. Tender.*)

CRAIG. When did Papa stop looking?

RICHARD. I don't know. The fifties? The sixties? Never?

CRAIG. Did he think about those Nicaragua papers? How close they got?

RICHARD. I don't know. I don't know. **I don't know!**

CRAIG. Dad, I brought you something.

RICHARD. My father was a hero. But I let fear stand in my way. I quit journalism. I couldn't ask any more questions. I saw Poland too late, with a young girl guide instead of my father, retracing steps from addresses on the backs of envelopes, like some murder mystery tour.

CRAIG. I guess it was a murder mystery tour.

RICHARD. Tell me about the slave letters.

CRAIG. Really?

RICHARD. I could use a pick-me-up.

CRAIG. Whoa. Um.

> (*Cogent and inspired.*) A couple months ago, I discovered a letter from a slave who was in the process of being repatriated to Africa. He was on board an

---

*A license to produce *The Book of Joseph* does not include a performance license for any third-party or copyrighted music. Licensees should create an original composition or use music in the public domain. For further information, please see Music Use Note on page 3.

illegal slave ship. The Americans find him and say, "Guess what, we're going to send you back to Africa!" And he writes this letter to the Secretary of the Navy saying, "I am *not African*. I am a *British subject*. I was kidnapped in the Caribbean and put on this ship, and I don't want to go back to Africa. I've *never been to Africa*."

RICHARD. Wow.

CRAIG. It took me weeks to decipher the handwriting. And I wish I got to know this gentleman further, but part of the tragic nature of slavery and the slave trade is that I don't get to make up anything else. I'll never be able to say, and then he went on with his life and he did this, he was gentle, he was kind. I don't know. All I've got is that scrap.

RICHARD. These were real people, and now they are gone.

CRAIG. My vision of heaven is you get all the answers and find out if you're right.

RICHARD. God you're young.

CRAIG. What do you mean?

RICHARD. I don't care who's right; I just want to see my parents again.

CRAIG. *(A discovery.)* Papa lost everyone, and so did you.

RICHARD. Me?

CRAIG. Dad, I came to give you this.

> *(Holds out his phone.)*

RICHARD. I still pay for that phone so technically it's already / mine.

CRAIG. Read.

RICHARD. Read it for me. The damn screen.

CRAIG. Facebook Messenger:

"Craig.

I am the son of Arnold Spitzman. I am sure the name is familiar to you. He immigrated as your grandfather's ward in 1939.

I would very much like to get in touch with you and your father Richard. My father is eighty-four, in decent health, and would also like to talk. He lived most of his life in Brazil and now he and my mother are in Florida.

Please respond as soon as possible.

Nicholas Spitzman."

RICHARD. The kid on the boat? In the court?

CRAIG. Dad, Arnold Spitzman made it! He's alive!

RICHARD. Why would he write to you and not me?

CRAIG. Because I'm on Facebook. You want to go meet him? In Destin, Florida? Only three flights and an eighty-mile drive.

RICHARD. Oh, I don't know...

CRAIG. Dad, would you like to come with?

> (**RICHARD** *takes* **CRAIG***'s hand. We shift to the modest Florida home or yard of Arnold Spitzman. A box of Vosges chocolates sits on the table.*)
>
> (*Arnold's wife,* **IRIS**, *stands near him.* **ELDERLY ARNOLD** *speaks intimately. He is full of life, in his way.*)

ELDERLY ARNOLD. A lot of things happened by luck.

I found a dime on the boat, my first American money. Mr. Hollander said keep it. For luck.

You had no choice, you want to live or you want to die. You want to live, you have to take what's coming. You know how it is, you study, go out with a girl, get involved with sports, I was involved with sports, a soccer player. A soccer player – I was European so I knew how to play, that's all.

I played at the Bronx Science High School. I have as much scientific mind as that bird in the yard but they felt sorry for me and let me in. My life was full, I make friends very very easily, I *made* anyway.

IRIS. *(Whisper to* **CRAIG** *and* **RICHARD**, *Latin accent.)* Maybe you can tell me why he is the way he is.

ELDERLY ARNOLD. What it amounts to is, I don't get involved too deeply in most of my life.

Since I married Iris, I don't need anybody in my life. She's my sister, she's my mother, she's my lover. And my son Nicholas, I don't have to say the obvious, I mean.

IRIS. *(Whisper.)* He has two daughters from his first marriage; they don't talk.

ELDERLY ARNOLD. You're looking at a self-made man in Nicholas, one hundred percent. He paid for his own education. I am a terrible businessman. A great salesman, but a terrible businessman.

I went to his Yale graduation a few years ago; Nicholas was called to the stage at least four or five times. Tremendous.

He finds me after, I'm crying my eyes out. He's so confused. I say, "I wish they'd all been here to see it, but they died in a concentration camp."

(Pause.)

Did you see my chair? That's my chair, that's where I do a lot of thinking and crying.

Lately I've found something very strange about me. I enjoy crying. I sometimes look for moments to weep. I go so far as to say that I may find pleasure in crying. European Jewish sentimentality that finally comes out in me.

(Pause.)

Until the age of thirteen I had a stamp collection, and I took it with me on the boat with the Hollanders. I kept it in the foster home. And when I left high school in my junior year I wanted a winter coat, a nice suit. I sold the stamp collection. If I told you for how much... forty dollars.

(Chuckles.)

Forty dollars. And I got my coat and suit. I even remember the name of the place. Liberty Stamps. I'm sure they're not there. Liberty Stamps on Liberty Street, Downtown.

Your father Joseph Hollander was a hero. He saved my life. He was a good human being, a mensch in every sense.

Just like his son.

(He eats a chocolate.)

Thank you. These are lovely.

*(**RICHARD** and **CRAIG** journey home.)*

*(In the 1940s, **JOSEPH** holds his briefcase.)*

JOSEPH. If it will happen that I will not have anything to leave to our children I will give them those first letters.

RICHARD. Joseph Hollander. A man who saw what was coming, made the leap, helped others across, and lived to tell the tale.

CRAIG. But never told the tale.

RICHARD. He never even said their names.

CRAIG. That was your job.

RICHARD. Our job.

CRAIG. Whose job?

RICHARD. Pray God you get a job.

*(They fist bump, **RICHARD** awkwardly.)*

*(We see the **KRAKOW FAMILY**, as they were at the first party in 1939, well-dressed and healthy. **RICHARD** sees each one, and perhaps each sees him back. It heals something.)*

Mania Nachtigall.

Salo Nachtigall.

Klara and Dawid Wimisner.

Genka Wimisner.

Lusia Wimisner.

Dola Blaustein.

Berta Hollander.

*(Somewhere, now, a slightly older **CRAIG** teaches new children their history.)*

(Meanwhile, **RICHARD** *watches* **JOSEPH** *with love and longing.)*

CRAIG. Say these names. Mania.

CHILD'S VOICE. Mania.

CRAIG. Salo.

CHILD'S VOICE. Salo.

CRAIG. Klara.

CHILD'S VOICE. Klara.

CRAIG. Genka.

CHILD'S VOICE. Genka.

CRAIG. Lusia.

CHILD'S VOICE. Lusia.

CRAIG. Dola.

CHILD'S VOICE. Dola.

CRAIG. Berta.

CHILD'S VOICE. Berta.

(Finally, **RICHARD** *addresses his father:)*

RICHARD. Joseph Hollander.

JOSEPH. Joseph Hollander.

(Lights fade. **RICHARD** *and* **JOSEPH** *illuminated together.)*

RICHARD. Dad?

*(***JOSEPH*** sees* **RICHARD** *fully. Their eyes meet. So much love.)*

I have a couple questions? While I've got you?

End of Play

CPSIA information can be obtained
at www.ICGtesting.com
Printed in the USA
LVHW022357260323
742666LV00012B/405

9 780573 707520